For Darcy and Teddy—I love you more than all the balloons in all the world —A. B.

For Rebecca Sherman —S. M.

SIMON & SCHUSTER BOOKS FOR YOUNG READERS
An imprint of Simon & Schuster Children's Publishing Division
1230 Avenue of the Americas, New York, New York 10020
Text copyright © 2017 by Ariel Bernstein
Illustrations copyright © 2017 by Scott Magoon
SIMON & SCHUSTER BOOKS FOR YOUNG READERS is a trademark of Simon & Schuster, Inc.
For information about special discounts for bulk purchases, please contact Simon & Schuster Special Sales at 1-866-506-1949 or business@simonandschuster.com.
The Simon & Schuster Speakers Bureau can bring authors to your live event. For more information or to book an event, contact the Simon & Schuster Speakers Bureau at 1-866-248-3049 or visit our website at www.simonspeakers.com.
Book design by Chloë Foglia
The text for this book was set in Geometric 415.
The illustrations for this book were rendered digitally.
Manufactured in China
0717 SCP
First Edition
2 4 6 8 10 9 7 5 3 1
CIP data for this book is available from the Library of Congress.
ISBN 978-1-4814-7250-0
ISBN 978-1-4814-7251-7 (eBook)

I HAVE A BALLOON

Written by Ariel Bernstein

Illustrated by Scott Magoon

A Paula Wiseman Book
Simon & Schuster Books for Young Readers
New York London Toronto Sydney New Delhi

I have a balloon.

You have a balloon.

I have a balloon.

That is a **big** balloon.

I have a **big** balloon.

That is a
shiny
red
balloon.

I have a
shiny
red
balloon.

That red balloon matches
my shiny red tie.

I'd look fancy walking to school
with a shiny red balloon.

The only thing I've ever wanted,
since right now,

is a shiny, big red balloon.

It would make me SO HAPPY!

I have
a teddy bear!

That is nice.
I have a balloon.

Do you want to trade with me?

No.

My sunflower is taller than your balloon!

Want to trade?

You have
a sock?

I have
a
sock.

Your sock has
a **star** on it.

Yes, my sock has
a star on it.

Your sock has a **hole** in it.
A **perfectly shaped hole**.

The sock does have a hole.
A **perfectly shaped hole**.

All I can do with my balloon is hold it.
All day.

Just standing here,
holding it.

You can wear a sock on your tail or your foot
or your hand or your ear.

You can make a sock puppet and play.

I will trade you your sock with a star
and a perfectly shaped hole
for my balloon.

You will trade me my sock
for your balloon?

My sock with a star
and a perfectly shaped hole?

Yes.

The star on my sock matches the star on my hat.
I'd look fancy walking to school wearing my sock.

I can wear my sock on my tail or my foot or my hand or my ear.

I can make a sock puppet and play.

All I've ever wanted,
since right now,
is a **sock** with a **star**
and a
perfectly shaped hole.

It makes me SO HAPPY!

whee!

You have a sock.

I have a sock.
You have a balloon.

I have a balloon.

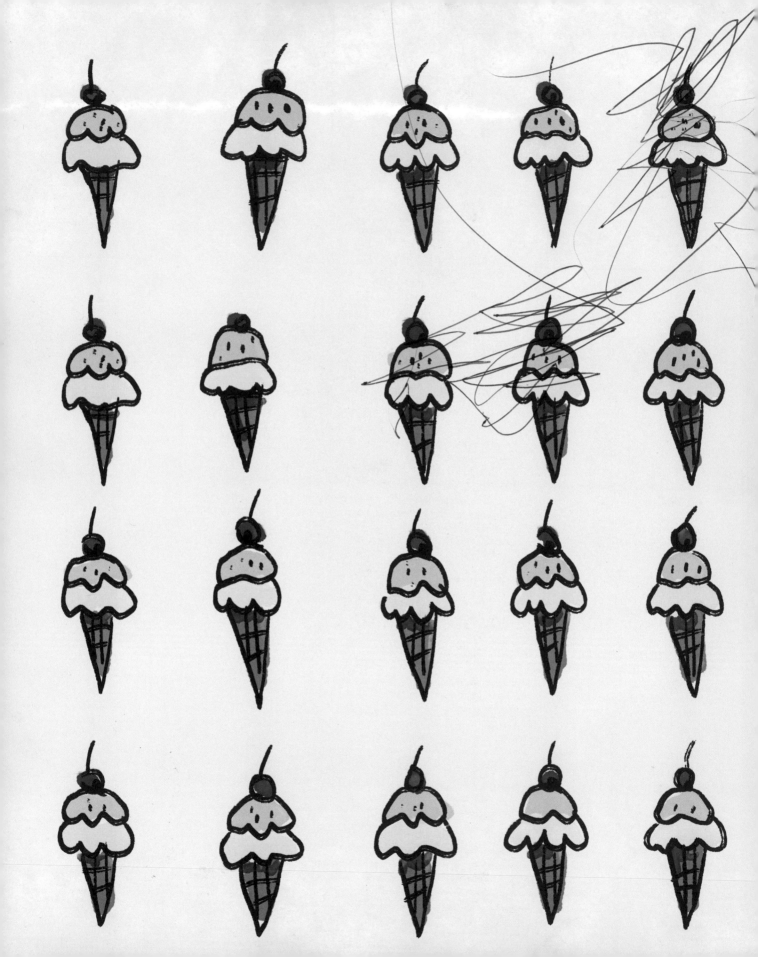